The Story of
Clan MacWee

(The smallest clan in Scotland)

Alison Mary Fitt & Willie Ritchie

First published in Great Britain 2008
Reprinted 2011

Design – Melvin Creative
Printing – Printer Trento, Italy

Published by
GW Publishing
PO Box 6091
Thatcham
Berks
RG19 8XZ.

Tel + 44 (0)1635 268080
www.gwpublishing.com

The Story of
Clan MacWee

(The smallest clan in Scotland)

If Scots words are new to you turn over and look,
you'll find them explained at the back of the book!

Publishing

Many years ago, so the story goes, a strange bunch of people lived in a dark and gloomy Scottish glen. They were known as Clan MacWee, because most of them were no taller than the thistles which grew around their front doors.

The reason they were so small was that for hundreds of years a great muckle black cloud had hung over Glen Wee. So in all that time there hadn't been any sun to make them, or their ancestors, grow. Every morning the Clan Chief, who was called Sma Sandy, shook his fist at it and yelled, "Go away you horrible black cloud."
But of course, it didn't!

They had tried **very** hard to get rid of it! Recently, they had hired the pipe band from Glen Skirl, hoping that the wind from their bag-pipes would blow the cloud away.

But although the pipers huffed, puffed and blew until they had no puff left, the cloud hadn't budged.

Then one day, some of the clansmen found a mouldy old canon, which had been left behind at one time by invaders from the South.

"Now we can fire boulders at that rotten old cloud, and break it up once and for all," they chuckled.

Well, that's what they hoped! But the first boulder they fired soared up in the air...

The second boulder they fired didn't reach the cloud either.
Instead, it walloped down with a muckle THUMP! in the heather,
and woke millions of midgies who had been having their morning nap.

The midgies weren't long in taking revenge!

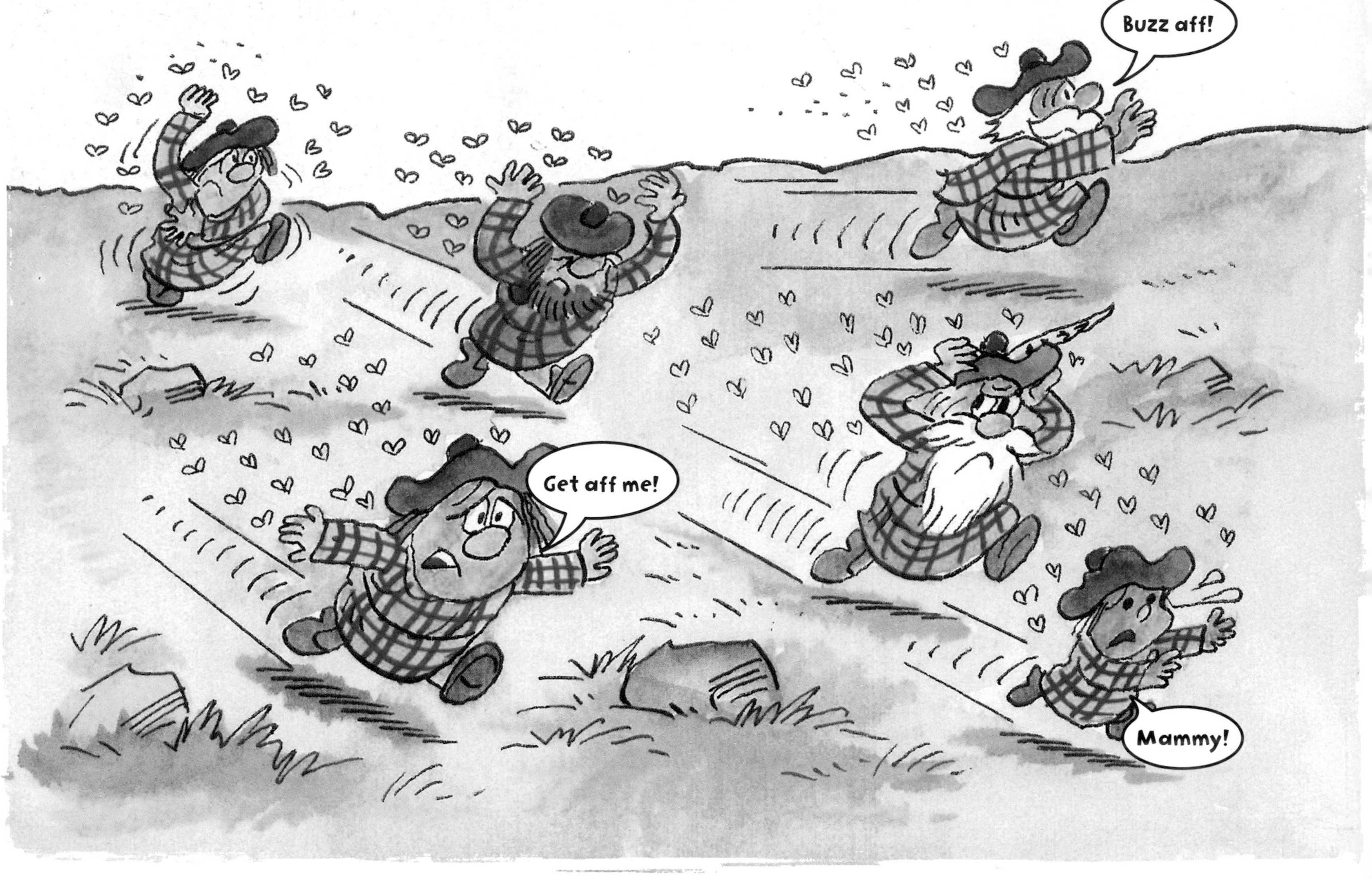

The clansmen who had fired the canon said they were very sorry for the trouble they had caused.

"So you should be," spluttered Sma Sandy, who was slathered in porridge. "I like to EAT my breakfast, not WEAR it! And thanks to you, half the clan are covered in midgie bites!"

He wasn't too mad at them, though. After all, they had only been trying to shift the cloud they all wanted rid of. But it looked as if it was never going to move!

There was nothing for it but to try some other ways of growing tall. First they held stretching classes, hoping they could **stretch** themselves taller.

But when they finally measured themselves, they hadn't grown at all. Not one teeny bit! They were so disappointed their faces were almost as long as their kilts. "After all our efforts," they muttered.

Then one morning, Sma Sandy climbed onto his upturned porridge pot and rallied his clansmen. "Do not lose heart," he told them stoutly. "Let us go into the next glen and see if there is any sun **there** that will make us grow."

You're on, Chief!

They all thought it was a great idea!

So they set off hopefully. Of course, they were soon tripping on their kilts and falling flat on their faces, so it took them ages to climb the brae out of Glen Wee.

At last they reached the top and there, blazing down on them was the sun. The MacWees gaped in amazement. Some had thought the sun was square. Some had argued that it was oblong. And some had even thought it was green with purple stripes! But there it was, up in the sky, big, round, yellow and very warm.

But what the MacWees didn't know was that the glen they were in was called Glen Muckle. And the people who lived there belonged to Clan Muckle. It was called that because for hundreds of years, the sun had shone down there and made everyone grow very tall indeed!

GLEN MUCKLE

Size 20 boots!

Tumble!

Hurry, lads!

Skite!

As they rushed away, they could hear the Muckle clansman's muckle hefty boots going THUMP! THUMP! as he chased after them. Of course, they were soon tripping over their kilts as usual. But for once they didn't mind, because it made them tumble down the hill faster than they could run.

That's because they were hiding from him!
And do you know what? There and then, the MacWees
decided that being wee wasn't such a bad thing to be after all.
In fact, it was a brilliant thing to be, because they could
tuck themselves away in all sorts of nooks and crannies!

Some words you need to know...

wee	means small
sma	means small too!
no'	is what Scots say for not
bide	means stay
cowp	means fall
blaw	means blow
fowk	are people
daylicht	is daylight
jist	means just
haud	means hold
lugs	means ears (annoying things you have to wash behind)
didna	is a Scots version of didn't

Sma Sandy explains...

fitba	that's a football
numptie	means idiot (careful who you call that!)
muckle	means large
stane	is a stone
aff	is what Scots might say for off
airms	are arms
abodie	means everyone
cannie	means be careful
jine	means join
wha	is Scots for who
mair	means more
drooned	is a Scots word for drowned
mak	is make
backerties	means backwards
braw	means great
nyaff	means a small impudent person (don't use this too often either!)
rin	means run
oot	means out
skite	is a Scots word for slip or slide
shooglie	means wobbly